KV-112-980

CONTENTS

Chapter 1

TO THE FAIREST

Aphrodite was the Greek goddess of love and beauty. One of the main myths about Aphrodite takes place during a celebration of love, which she attended. A joyous event was about to take place on Mount Pelion. King Peleus was marrying a sea **nymph** called Thetis. All the Greek gods and goddesses were invited to the wedding except Eris, the goddess of **discord**. She became furious when she found out and decided to get revenge by causing trouble. So she threw a golden apple into the crowd. On the fruit she had written the words "To the Fairest".

Three goddesses claimed the gift. Hera was the wife of Zeus and queen of all the gods and goddesses. She was sure the apple was meant for her. Athena was the goddess of wisdom. She knew that no one was more beautiful than she was. She could not imagine that the gift could be for anyone but her. But Aphrodite was the goddess of love. She was a great beauty, herself. She too claimed the apple and the title of the fairest.

APHRODITE

GREEK GODDESS OF LOVE AND BEAUTY

by Tammy Gagne

Raintree is an imprint of Capstone Global Library Limited, a company incorporated in England and Wales having its registered office at 264 Banbury Road, Oxford, OX2 7DY – Registered company number: 6695582

www.raintree.co.uk
myorders@raintree.co.uk

Edited by Gina Kammer
Designed by Bobbie Nuytten
Original illustrations © Capstone Global Library Limited 2020
Picture research by Svetlana Zhurkin
Production by Katy LaVigne
Originated by Capstone Global Library Ltd
Printed and bound in India

ISBN 978 1 4747 9016 1 (hardback)
ISBN 978 1 4747 9021 5 (paperback)

British Library Cataloguing in Publication Data
A full catalogue record for this book is available from the British Library.

Acknowledgements
We would like to thank the following for permission to reproduce photographs: Alamy: Chronicle, 7, Prisma Archivo, cover, Science History Images, 29 (top); Bridgeman Images: Museum of Fine Arts, Houston, Texas, USA/Gift of Miss Annette Finnigan/Victoriatus with Zeus and Dione on obverse and thunderbolt in wreath with legend on reverse, 238-168 BC (silver), Greek School, (3rd-2nd century BC), 12; Getty Images: DEA/A. Dagli Orti, 14, DEA/G. Dagli Orti, 5, Mondadori Portfolio, 25 (bottom left); Newscom: akg-images, 8, 22, 27 (bottom), 29 (bottom), Album/Fine Art Images, 16, 27 (top), Heritage Images/Art Media, 9 (top), Heritage Images/London Metropolitan Archives/City of London, 20, Heritage Images/The Print Collector, 21; Shutterstock: Debu55y, 28, Elena Efimova, 4, EleniKa, 25 (top), Gala_Kan, 17, John_Silver, 24, LeniKovaleva, 10, leoks, 26, Maksimilian, 11, Mark Lijesen, 15, Masterrr, 18, 19, Sanit Fuangnakhon, 9 (bottom), Stavrida, 25 (bottom right), Yakov Oskanov, 13

Design Elements by Shutterstock

The three beautiful goddesses, Hera, Athena and Aphrodite, await judgement by Paris to find out who is fairest among them.

Eris had accomplished her goal. The guests were not focused on the happy couple. Instead, they could not stop watching the fight for the golden apple. When the three goddesses couldn't work it out themselves, they turned to Zeus. But the king of the gods wanted nothing to do with the decision. He did not want to be the one to anger two of the women in his family by choosing only one of the three. He turned the decision over to Paris, a **mortal** prince of Troy.

nymph minor female goddess who lives on earth
discord lack of agreement; conflict
mortal human, referring to a being who will eventually die

A PROMISE OF LOVE LEADS TO WAR

Each of the goddesses believed herself to be the most beautiful. But all three goddesses still tried to bribe the young prince. Hera promised Paris great wealth and power if he gave the apple to her. Athena offered to make him victorious in war in exchange for the prize. Not to be outdone by the others, Aphrodite also made a promise. She told Paris that if he chose her, he would win the heart of the most beautiful mortal woman in the world. No one can say whether Paris made a fair decision. But he chose Aphrodite, and took her up on her offer of love.

GODDESS FACT

Greek and Roman myths tell the same basic stories. But the Romans gave the gods and goddesses different names. In Roman mythology, Aphrodite is known as Venus.

When Paris chose between the goddesses, he was living as a shepherd and did not yet know that he was a prince.

1

To Paris, the most beautiful mortal woman was Helen, the wife of the Spartan King Menelaus. Aphrodite helped the prince with a plan to kidnap the young queen so they could run away together. Menelaus responded by sending more than 1,000 ships to find his wife and bring her back. Under Aphrodite's influence, Paris's decisions led the people of Greece and Troy into the Trojan War.

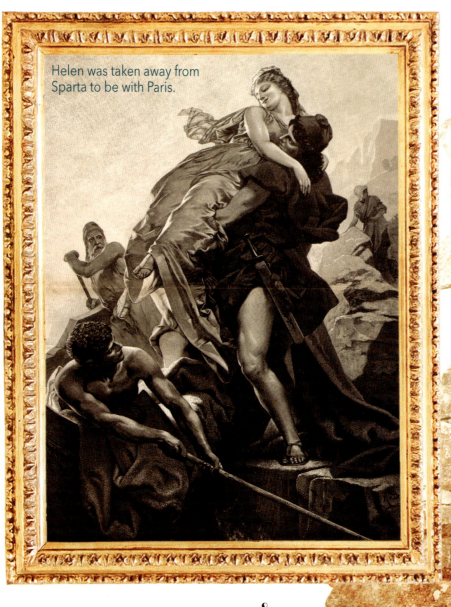

Helen was taken away from Sparta to be with Paris.

The goddess of love and beauty

In addition to being the goddess of love, Aphrodite was also the goddess of beauty. Many people in ancient Greece worshipped her. They hoped to be rewarded with great love of their own. Women thought worshipping Aphrodite would bring them children.

Aphrodite was also worshipped as a sea goddess. Sailors believed that she brought calm waters and safe travels. For this reason they often prayed to her before their voyages.

GODDESS FACT

Aphrodite's sacred animal is the dove. The goddess rode in a chariot pulled by doves. She is also linked with swans, and sometimes she is shown riding a swan.

Chapter 2

THE CREATION OF APHRODITE

Myths such as the story of the golden apple were important to the ancient Greeks. They believed that gods and goddesses controlled the world from the top of Mount Olympus. The oldest myths about Aphrodite say her father was Uranus, god of the sky. In these stories, Aphrodite has no mother. She is born from the foam of the sea as a fully formed adult. This all takes place two **generations** before Zeus himself is born. Then Uranus ruled the universe with his wife Gaia, the Earth goddess.

Aphrodite never knew her father. Uranus had other children before Aphrodite. But he did not love any of them. In fact, he hated them so much that he hid his oldest children away deep in the Earth. But Gaia wanted to free them. She gave her son Cronus a **sickle**. When Cronus attacked Uranus with this weapon, parts of his body fell into the ocean and became the foam from which Aphrodite was born.

Aphrodite is often shown rising from a shell, which symbolizes how she was born from the sea.

10

The ancient Greek poet Hesiod told this creation story about Aphrodite around 700 BC. According to Hesiod, Aphrodite floated past the island of Cytherea as foam. And she kept floating until she came to Cyprus. Once there, she walked ashore as a goddess. The ancient Greeks built a **temple** to honour Aphrodite on this island in the Mediterranean Sea. People throughout Greece worshipped Aphrodite.

generation   group of people born around the same time
sickle   long, curved blade attached to a short handle
temple   building used for worship

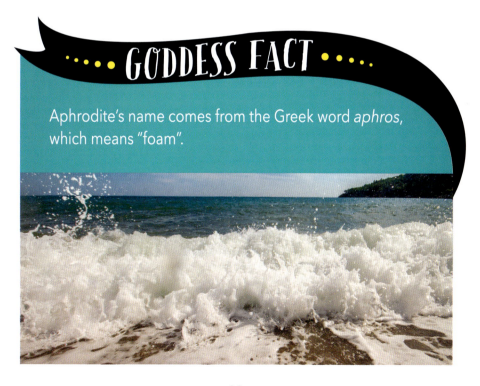

····· GODDESS FACT ·····

Aphrodite's name comes from the Greek word *aphros*, which means "foam".

A DIFFERENT BIRTH STORY

Some Greek myths tell the same story in different ways. Aphrodite's creation story is a perfect example of this. According to some Greek myths, Aphrodite did not come from sea foam. These stories state that her parents were Zeus and Dione. Dione was a Titan goddess – one of the first gods created by Gaia and Uranus, the gods of the earth and the sky. Her name is the female version of Dios, a form of the name Zeus. Although Zeus was married to Hera, some myths say Dione was Zeus's first wife.

The Greek poet Homer passed this version of Aphrodite's origins down to future generations of Greek people. He lived around the same time as Hesiod. Through their stories, Aphrodite and the other Greek gods eventually became known throughout the world.

Zeus and Dione

GODDESS FACT

Because of the myths in which Aphrodite is said to be the daughter of Dione, Aphrodite is sometimes called Dionaea, a form of her mother's name.

The origins of Aphrodite

Although different cultures have similar gods and goddesses, each one is a bit different. Aphrodite is part of the Greek **pantheon**. But similar forms of the goddess also exist in other cultures. Aphrodite is also identified with the Phoenician goddess Astarte, the Babylonian goddess Ishtar and the Egyptian goddess Isis. Astarte was also her culture's goddess of heaven and war.

Aphrodite is different from the other goddesses found in the Mediterranean, though. She rules mainly over love.

pantheon all the gods of a particular mythology

Egyptian goddess Isis

13

Chapter 3

APHRODITE AND HER FAMILY

Aphrodite had no full brothers or sisters. But as the daughter of Zeus she had many half-siblings. They included her half-brothers Apollo, Ares and Hermes. She also had several half-sisters, including Artemis, Athena and Persephone.

Among the gods in Greek mythology, many brothers and sisters had romantic relationships. This was the case for Aphrodite and Ares. But Aphrodite was already the wife of Hephaistos, the god of fire. Much like her father, and many other gods, Aphrodite was often unfaithful to her spouse.

Aphrodite and Ares

When Hephaistos found out that Aphrodite and Ares had fallen in love, he made a plan to catch them together. He made it look like he was leaving on a journey. He then hid while he waited for Ares to come to Aphrodite. As soon as he did, Hephaistos dropped a large net on the pair. It trapped them so the other gods and goddesses could see what Aphrodite and Ares had done.

Hephaistos hoped the other gods and goddesses would shame the couple. But Aphrodite's beauty was so great that at least one god defended them. Hermes, the messenger god, admitted to everyone that he would do anything to win the love of the stunning goddess.

When the other gods saw Aphrodite's affair with Ares, Aphrodite was embarrassed. But Poseidon, the god of the sea, comforted her. The two soon fell in love. They had a daughter together called Rhodos. She became the goddess of the island of Rhodes.

Hermes

GODDESS FACT

Hermes fell in love with Aphrodite too. It led to their child, Hermaphroditus.

APHRODITE'S MANY CHILDREN

The Greek goddess of love had more than twelve children. Several of them were the result of her relationship with Ares. Their sons, Phobos and Deimos, often went to war alongside their father. Phobos was the god of fear. Deimos was the god of terror. Their talents helped Ares get the advantage even before the battles began. Their daughter, Harmonia, was the goddess of harmony. She was the opposite of Eris, the goddess of strife and discord.

Aphrodite is often pictured with one or more of the Erotes around her. The Erotes were winged gods and goddesses of love. In some myths, Aphrodite is called their mother. Of the Erotes, Eros was the god of passion. His twin, Himeros, was the god of desire. Pothos was the god of longing. Their other brother Anteros was the god of mutual love.

Aphrodite and one of the Erotes

GODDESS FACT

One of Aphrodite's human lovers was a Trojan shepherd called Anchises. They had a son together called Aeneas.

Aphrodite and Adonis

Aphrodite was drawn to beautiful people. As soon as she saw the handsome infant Adonis, she decided he was meant to be hers. She hid him in a chest and asked Persephone to look after him. But when Persephone looked at the baby, she wanted him for herself. She refused to return him to her half-sister.

Aphrodite and Persephone argued about the matter until Zeus finally stepped in. He asked a **muse** called Calliope to decide the child's fate. Calliope declared that Adonis would spend half of each year with Aphrodite and the other half with Persephone.

muse goddess of song, poetry, arts and science in Greek mythology

17

Aphrodite's family tree

The goddess of love and beauty had many relationships and many children. Aphrodite's own birth myths have a couple of different versions that add even more possible family ties. Her family tree shows some of the important connections Aphrodite had to other gods and even humans.

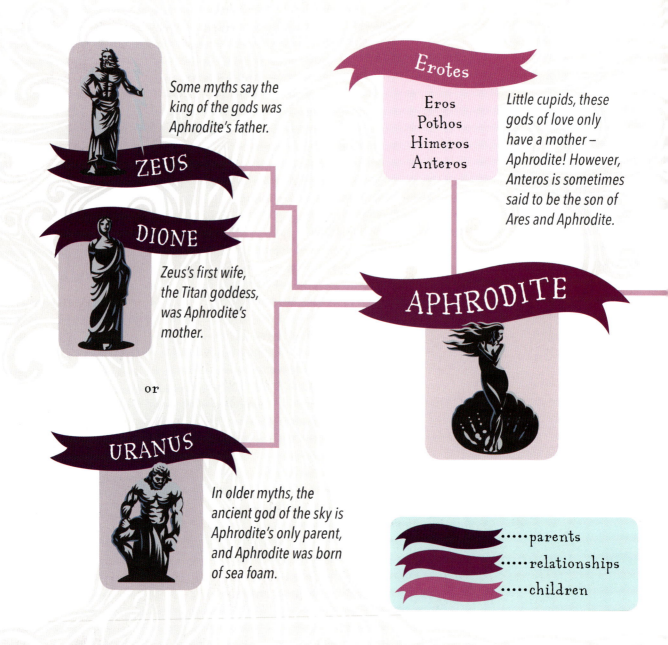

Some myths say the king of the gods was Aphrodite's father.

ZEUS

DIONE

Zeus's first wife, the Titan goddess, was Aphrodite's mother.

or

URANUS

In older myths, the ancient god of the sky is Aphrodite's only parent, and Aphrodite was born of sea foam.

Erotes

Eros
Pothos
Himeros
Anteros

Little cupids, these gods of love only have a mother – Aphrodite! However, Anteros is sometimes said to be the son of Ares and Aphrodite.

APHRODITE

···· parents
···· relationships
···· children

18

Aphrodite's husband was the god of fire. They had no children together.

HEPHAISTOS

Aphrodite had two sons with the god of war. Phobos and Deimos were the gods of fear and terror. Their daughter, Harmonia, was the goddess of harmony.

ARES

Phobos

Deimos

Harmonia

The messenger god had one son with Aphrodite. Hermaphroditus looked similar to the winged Erotes.

HERMES

Hermaphroditus

POSEIDON

Rhodos

With the god of the sea, Aphrodite had a daughter. Rhodos was the goddess of the island of Rhodes.

Aphrodite loved a human man called Anchises. Their son, Aeneas, became a hero of the Trojan War.

ANCHISES

Aeneas

Chapter 4

APHRODITE'S POWERS AND WEAKNESSES

Like all gods, Aphrodite was immortal. She also had the ability to inspire love wherever she went. Gods and men alike couldn't help but fall in love with Aphrodite because of her great beauty. But she was also capable of making gods and mortals fall in love with one another. Aphrodite could make the ordinary seem spectacular.

Aphrodite was known for having a magic girdle. This piece of clothing was said to make everyone desire the goddess. In one myth, Hera borrowed the girdle to get the romantic attention of Zeus. The girdle inspired love and desire for its wearer.

GODDESS FACT

In one myth, Aphrodite's magic girdle was stolen by Helen's servant.

Hera borrows Aphrodite's magic girdle. Sometimes she borrowed it to give to others to help stop married couples fighting.

The ancient Greeks often looked to Aphrodite for help with their love lives. They wanted to feel special. And they knew she had the power to make that happen. Young brides asked for her help to make their weddings happy occasions. They also thought she could help their new marriages go well.

In some ways Aphrodite was even more powerful than Zeus. Although he was the king of all the gods, she led him into many of his love affairs with humans. Her power to affect Zeus's emotions angered him. He was also embarrassed when the other gods laughed at him for having relationships with humans. The gods saw themselves as being better than humans. In one myth Zeus got revenge on Aphrodite by forcing her to fall in love with the human Anchises.

Aphrodite falls in love with Anchises while he herds cattle. Dressed beautifully, she claimed to be a mortal princess. Aphrodite made even the animals she saw fall in love with each other.

APHRODITE'S DOWNFALL

Aphrodite's beauty and powers made her one of the mightiest goddesses. But like the other gods, she had her share of faults. One of them was her **vanity**. It was not just others who saw Aphrodite as the most beautiful goddess. She began to see herself that way, too, and she focused too much on what her looks could get her.

Aphrodite thought that she deserved everything and everyone she wanted. She was jealous of anyone who was also seen as attractive. And when she did not get her way, she became **vengeful**. Although she had the ability to inspire love, she spent much of her time causing others pain and discontent.

Aphrodite was often shown with mirrors to represent her vanity.

vanity extreme pride in one's appearance or achievements

vengeful wanting revenge

One of the ways Aphrodite hurt others was through her disloyalty. She fell in love quickly and often. On many occassions she chose the next object of her affection while she was still involved with another god or man. Many of them knew that she was unlikely to be faithful. But her immense beauty made them think she was worth the trouble.

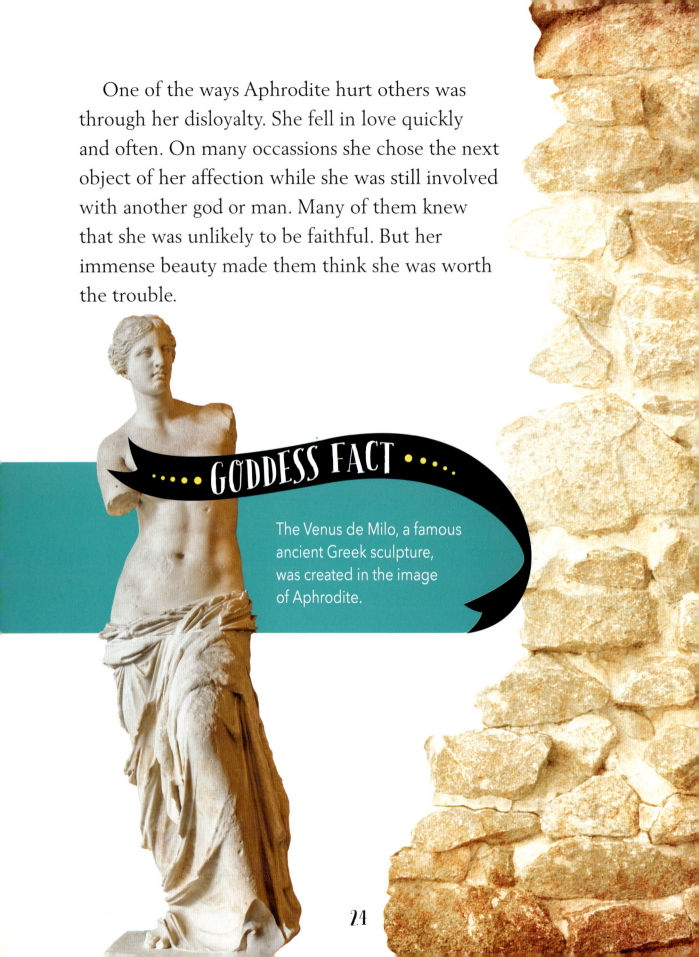

GODDESS FACT

The Venus de Milo, a famous ancient Greek sculpture, was created in the image of Aphrodite.

What did Aphrodite look like?

Like the other Greek gods and goddesses, Aphrodite looked like a human. The ancient Greeks saw her as the ideal female. She was the highest symbol of physical beauty.

Artwork of Aphrodite usually showed her as a young woman. She had **delicate** features and was always smiling. In many paintings and statues, Aphrodite was nude. But she was also shown in elegant robes and jewellery.

delicate small and fine

Chapter 5

APHRODITE IN GREEK HISTORY AND MODERN CULTURE

Myths about Aphrodite linked her to Cyprus. This island played a large role in her origin story. Many ancient Greeks also believed that this was where the goddess lived when she spent time on Earth. Festivals were held on the island in honour of the goddess of love.

Cyprus is an island in the Mediterranean Sea.

For many years, stories of Aphrodite and the other Greek gods were passed down by word of mouth. Homer was the man credited with playing a large part in shaping their stories. He told these stories in the *Iliad* and the *Odyssey*. These poems from the 700s BC explain Aphrodite's origin. They also tell how the goddess of love became the wife of Hephaistos and the lover of Ares. Aphrodite came to stand for much more than beauty among both the Greeks and Romans. She also became a symbol of the passion and creativity that often goes with love. This image focused much more on the positive aspects of the goddess than the negative ones.

A 17th century artist's depiction of the poet Homer

GODDESS FACT

The Roman poet Lucretius called the goddess Genetrix. This mother figure stood for the spring, birth and creativity.

APHRODITE'S MODERN FOLLOWERS

Aphrodite remains a major symbol of love and beauty in modern Greece and around the world. She is known far beyond the borders of her native land. The temple built for her on Cyprus has stood in ruins for more than 2,100 years. But people still travel to this famous site. Some even leave offerings for Aphrodite – just like the ancient Greeks did thousands of years ago.

The myths that brought Aphrodite to life for the ancient Greeks are also still told throughout the world. Stories about her even appear in modern fiction, such as Rick Riordan's *Percy Jackson* book series. Whether she is called Aphrodite or Venus, the goddess of love will truly live forever.

GODDESS FACT

One of the temples of Aphrodite is located in the city of Athens. It is called Temple of Aphrodite Urania.

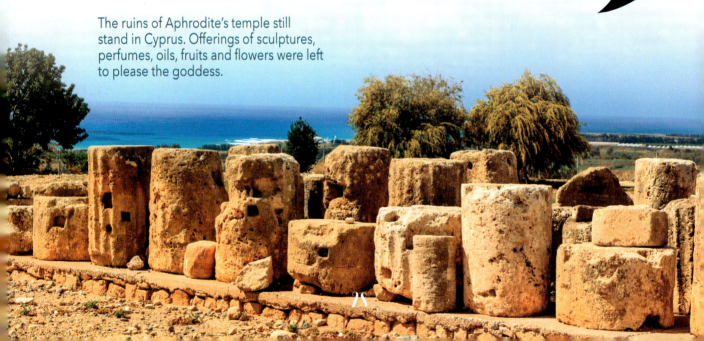

The ruins of Aphrodite's temple still stand in Cyprus. Offerings of sculptures, perfumes, oils, fruits and flowers were left to please the goddess.

one of the Erotes

Aphrodite

doves, sacred animals

chariot pulled by doves

Did that really happen?

Most myths include some fantastic events. Humans have never seen many of the things that take place in these stories. Picturing Aphrodite being born from foam floating on water requires imagination.

Many people in ancient Greece believed myths were true stories. Some people today also believe these events really happened. But others see them as stories created to teach lessons. Whichever is the case, Greek mythology remains an important part of Greek culture.

An ancient water jug shows a scene from the myth known as the Judgement of Paris.

GLOSSARY

delicate small and fine

discord lack of agreement; conflict

generation group of people born around the same time

immortal able to live forever

mortal human, referring to a being who will eventually die

muse goddess of song, poetry, arts and science in ancient Greek mythology

nymph minor female goddess who lives on Earth

pantheon all the gods of a particular mythology

sickle long, curved blade attached to a short handle

temple building used for worship

vanity extreme pride in one's appearance or achievements

vengeful wanting revenge

FIND OUT MORE

BOOKS

Ancient Greece (Eyewitness), DK (DK Children, 2014)

Ancient Greece (History Hunters), Nancy Dickmann (Raintree, 2017)

Greek Myths and Legends (All About Myths), Jilly Hunt (Raintree, 2015)

The Odyssey (Puffin Classics), Geraldine McCaughrean (Puffin Classics, 1997)

The Usborne Book of Greek Myths, Anna Milbourne and Louie Stowell (Usborne Publishing Ltd, 2010)

WEBSITES

www.bbc.com/bitesize/articles/zgt7mp3
Learn more about the gods and heroes from Greek mythology.

www.dkfindout.com/uk/history/ancient-greece/ancient-greek-gods-and-goddesses
Find out more about ancient Greek gods and goddesses.

INDEX